For Jessica,
& Monica,
Melissa,
Alice.

LITTLE RED RIDING HOOD

Illustrated by Gerda Neubacher
Retold by Dympna Hayes

Cyril Hayes Press Inc.
3312 Mainway, Burlington, Ontario L7M 1A7
One Colomba Drive, Niagara Falls,
New York 14305

Once there was a little girl whose grandmother loved her dearly. For her birthday her grandmother made a special red hood. "When you wear this red riding hood, always remember that you are strong and good," said her grandmother as she gave it to the girl.

The little girl wore the hood every day, and soon everyone called her Little Red Riding Hood.

One day, Little Red Riding Hood helped her mother bake some chocolate chip cookies. When the cookies were cooling on the countertop, the mother said to her daughter, "If you would like to give your grandmother a lovely surprise, I will pack up some of the cookies in your little basket. You wash your hands and face, brush your hair and put on your cosy red hood. Then you can go quickly over to Grandma's house to have milk and cookies with her."

Red Riding Hood thought this was a great idea, and as quick as a wink she was ready and off to visit her grandma. As she walked down the road to Grandma's house, she was surprised by a big gray wolf who jumped out of the woods beside the road and asked her, "What have you got in your basket, Little Red Riding Hood?"

"Cookies, Mr. Wolf. Chocolate chip cookies, and I'm going down to my grandma's house with them."

"Hmmm...," said the wolf, "I thought as much. In fact, I smelled as much. They're my favorite kind, you know. I wish I were Grandma."

While the wolf was talking, he was quickly making a plan in his head to trick the little girl into giving him the cookies.

"Well, good day, Little Red Riding Hood," he said, and ran off through the woods – straight to Grandma's house. He had planned to growl and try to scare the grandma away, but luckily she was out in the garden behind her little cottage, picking flowers.

"Great," thought the wolf, and he pulled Grandma's nightgown on and popped her nightcap over his big ears and slid down under the lovely patchwork quilt on Grandma's bed.

When Little Red Riding Hood came in and saw the wolf wearing her grandmother's clothes, she nearly laughed out loud. Instead, she decided to play the game and pretend along with the wolf.

"Grandmother," she said, "what big eyes you have."

"All the better to see you with, my dear," replied the wolf, in his best grandmother voice. "All the better to see those yummy cookies," he thought.

"Grandmother, what a big nose you have!" said Little Red Riding Hood.

"All the better to smell the flowers, my dear," replied the wolf. "All the better to smell the cookies," he thought.

"Grandmother, what big teeth you have," said Little Red Riding Hood.

"All the better to eat with, my dear, especially when I am going to eat a whole basket of chocolate chip cookies all by myself," shouted the wolf, as he jumped out of Grandma's bed.

Just then, Grandma came in from the garden with a beautiful, big bunch of flowers in her arms. When she saw the wolf she threw all the flowers at him and quickly grabbed the broom from the corner and chased him, helter skelter, out of the house.

Little Red Riding Hood laughed and laughed at the poor wolf. Her grandma enjoyed the adventure too, and they were still laughing about it as they enjoyed their milk and cookies together.

The End